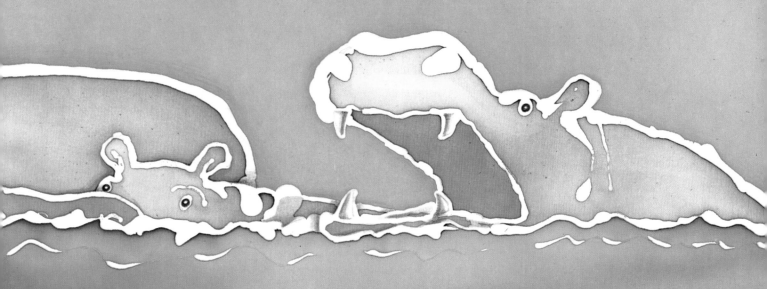

For Kate, Oliver, Emma, and Ruth

First published in the United States 1991 by Dial Books for Young Readers
A Division of Penguin Books USA Inc.
375 Hudson Street · New York, New York 10014

Published in Great Britain by Macmillan Children's Books
A Vanessa Hamilton Book
Copyright © 1990 by Patricia MacCarthy
All rights reserved · Printed in Great Britain
First Edition
N
1 3 5 7 9 10 8 6 4 2

Library of Congress Cataloging in Publication Data
MacCarthy, Patricia. Herds of words / Patricia MacCarthy.
p. cm.
Summary: Text and illustrations provide examples of named groups
of animals, people, and things, including a parliament of owls,
a crew of sailors, and a fleet of ships.
ISBN 0-8037-0892-0
1. English language—Collective nouns—Juvenile literature.
2. Vocabulary—Juvenile literature.   [1. English language—Collective nouns.
2. English language—Terms and phrases.   3. Vocabulary.] I. Title.
PE1689.M22 1991   428.1—dc20   90-31537 CIP AC

The art for this book consists of batik paintings on silk,
which were color-separated and reproduced in full color.

The title page of *Herds of Words* depicts *an ostentation of peacocks;*
the endpapers portray *a bloat of hippos.*

Herds of Words

Patricia MacCarthy

DIAL BOOKS FOR YOUNG READERS

New York

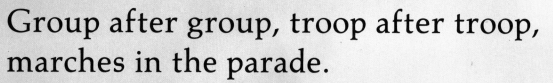

Group after group, troop after troop,
marches in the parade.
What is the word for each different herd
to star in this cavalcade:
A coven, a cloud, or a convocation,
a squadron, a sounder, an exaltation,
a run, leap, or stand, or an ostentation?

a husk of hares

a convocation of eagles

a sounder of swine

a fleet of ships

a crew of sailors

a huddle of walruses

a squadron of aircraft

a cavalcade of horsemen

a skein of geese

a bask of crocodiles

a stand of flamingos

a clutch of eggs

a charm of goldfinches

a wedge of swans

a hoard of treasure

a galaxy of stars

a coven of witches

a parliament of owls

a spring of teal

a covey of partridges

an exaltation of larks

a wisp of snipe

a cete of badgers

a cast of falcons

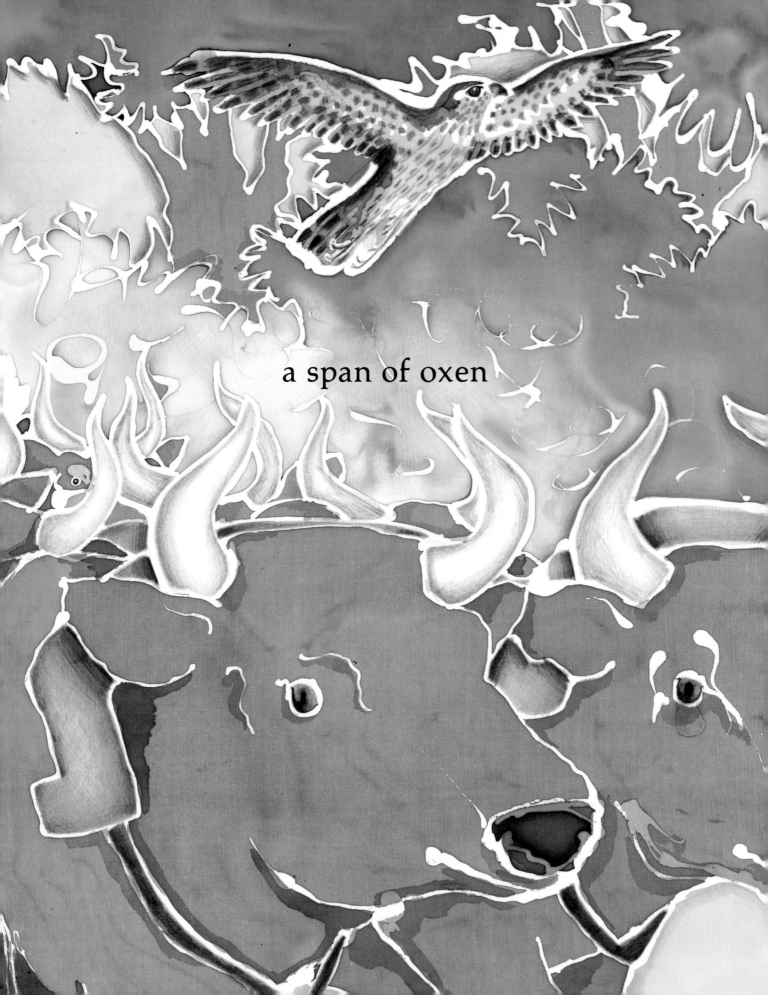

a span of oxen

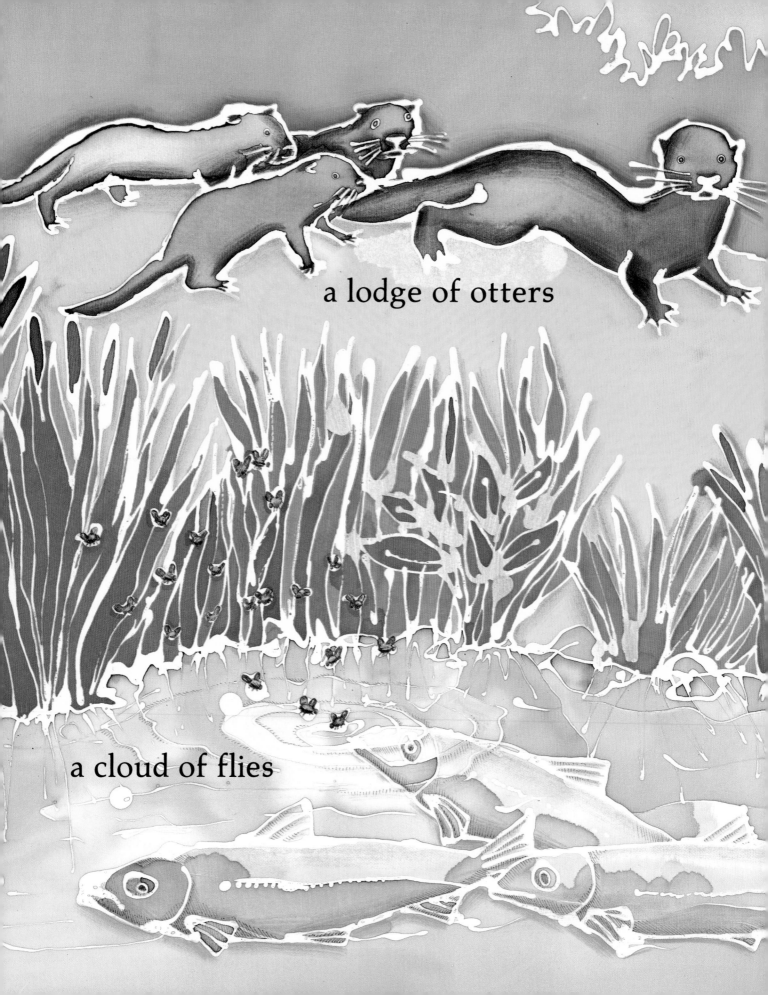

a lodge of otters

a cloud of flies

a run of salmon

a posse of constables

a dray of squirrels

a business of ferrets

a forest of trees

a pack of hounds

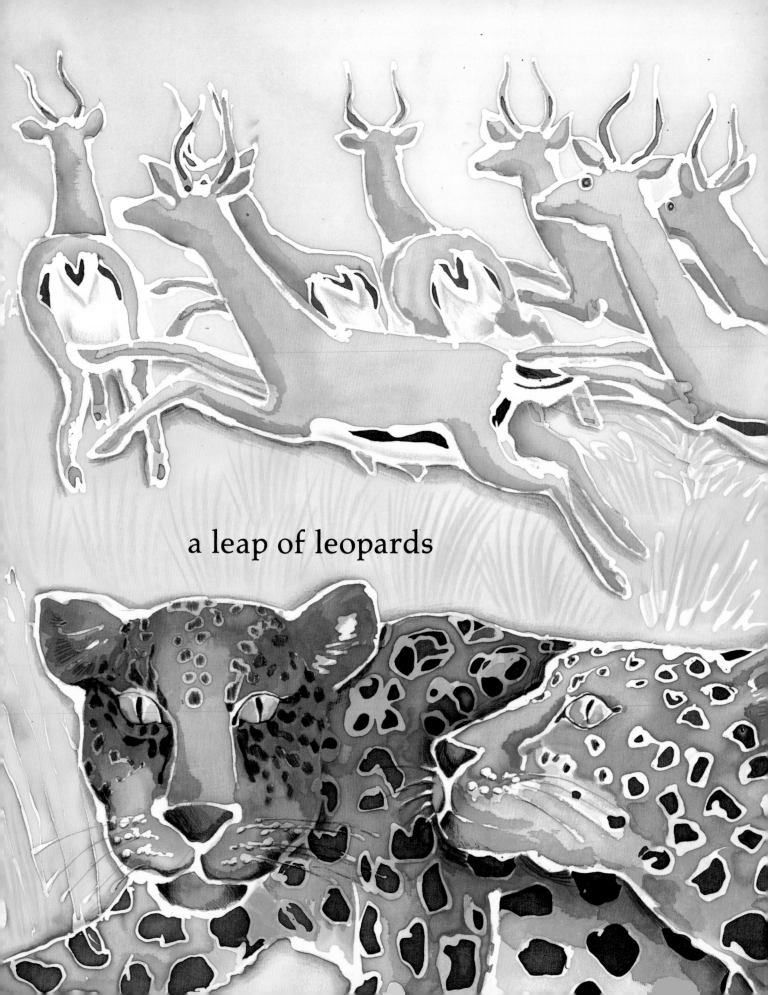

a leap of leopards

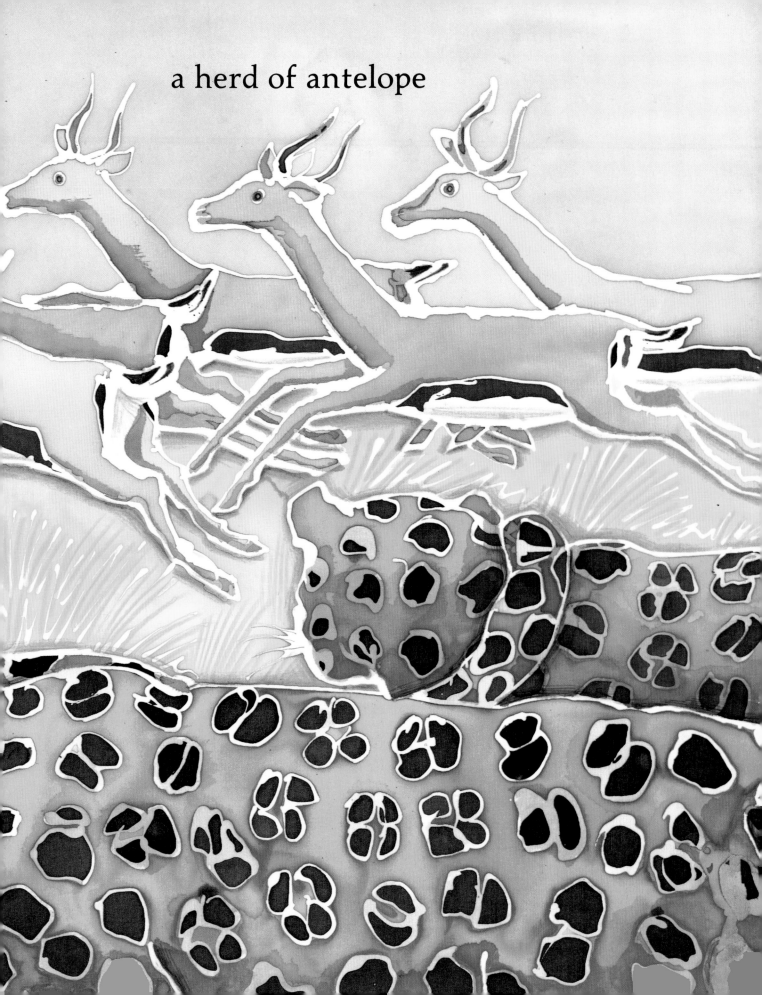

a herd of antelope

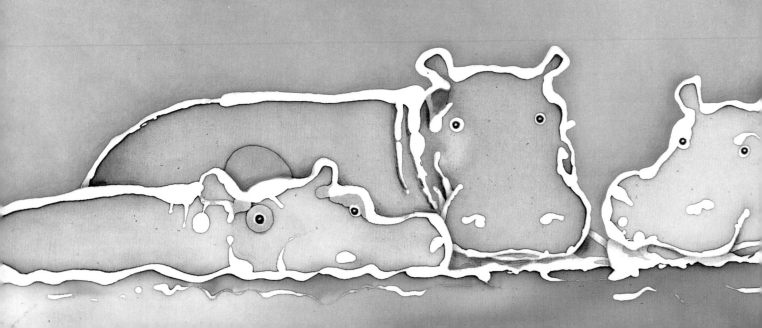